# MIND SEEKERS

BY DAVID G EVANS

# Table of Contents

The leader of the world, Sabastian wasn't happy with all the freedoms that people had.

In Europe he took over all the farmers land, to build chip manufacturing plants there. These chips are used in everything from cars to missiles.

If any of the farmers tried to fight back they would be killed by his mercenaries. Many of the farmers had several kids, and the future for them is looking awfully bleak.

Every farmer that lived in Europe was flown down to Mexico, to start their lives over. The farmers are to work on the many avocado farms, if they run off the avocado farms they'll be killed by

Sabastian's guards. Sabastian took away freedom of speech, a year later.

All of the social media platforms were taken down, nobody was allowed to start another social platform.

Whomever spoke out against him was assassinated, and not even buried. There were only 40 guns left in the whole entire world which belong to the elite's guards and Sabastian.

Under his rule Congress was forced to work on weekends, with no exceptions. When someone working in congress turns 78, they're allowed to retire and a new young congressional candidate gets voted on.

Sabastian is in power of the world for life, 3 assassination attempts were foiled by his well-trained personal security guards. His wife is deemed as the queen of the world.

Between her and Sabastian, they have 27 mansions all over the world, and 68 million in wealth. One of the mansions was broken into, but luckily nobody was home.

A famous painting was stolen, along with some expensive jewelry. This painting belonged to his mother, that she gave to him when he turned 19 years old. Growing up he always kept himself in good shape.

The first day that he was in power of the world, many of his good friends walked away from him saying that they never wanted to see him ever again.

In the backyard of his mansion, he paid a French sculptor 2 million to sculpt a lion made of marble. 2 days later the thieves that stole the painting and the jewelry were caught.

Nobody is allowed to be homeless, if someone is found living on the streets then they'll be forced to serve in the armed forces.

Sabastian ordered his military to take down every statue in North America. He even went so far to redesign the flag. Griffin aliens have taken over much of the Middle East.

Sabastian has lost 1,000 soldiers to fighting the aliens, the aliens attack using war flying saucers. The size of their attacking fleet is unknown at the moment, a hybrid human, who has 85% griffin DNA is a spy for the humans.

He blends in perfectly with the other aliens and they don't realize that he's partially human.

After a month of living alongside the aliens, he left and came to Sabastian's office. He shared with him that the alien stronghold was in Syria and Iraq. In Syria there are hundreds of aliens, just waiting to attack another human soldier.

They have 2 spacecraft that are used to defend the aliens that are fighting on the ground. The spacecrafts have 3 plasma cannons inside of them.

Sabastian's soldiers have successfully taken over Kuwait from the aliens. Inside the borders of Kuwait, the soldiers are setting up 2 different kinds of artillery pieces.

Among 3 hydro shock ray guns that can hit targets from 4 miles away with great precision.

They have one flying tank, but it's technology is outdated compared to what the aliens have and would make an easy target for the aliens.

For even more added protection, they placed an invisible cloak over the entire base. Even the soldiers carry new advanced weaponry, every new gun shoots a laser.

This allows the operator to shoot the gun infinitely, the internal laser system generates more laser every time it fires. With days of heavy fighting the soldiers were able to take back half of Iran.

They don't know how long they're defensive systems will hold out against the aliens. They gave Sabastian a call, he told them what they didn't want to hear.

Try to stay there and stand your ground for as long as you can. If it gets any worse get out of there.

The soldiers fired off 2 artillery pieces at once at one of the alien spacecraft, to counter strike the aliens.

On top of that they called in a drone strike, the troid drones fired galactic express drone missiles.

The drone missiles were able to go through places that they could never get to before. When the missiles hit their target and detonated the explosion was so intense that it left a crater, 15 of the aliens were blown to pieces.

## Chapter 1

Many months later the soldiers were able to take over 4 more countries in the Middle East.

Sabastian’s compound was attacked by 3 rogue aliens, his mercenaries were able to take out the threat.

The one world Air Force is called Superior Air. The fighter jets are 8th generation and controlled by artificial intelligence with no purpose to use a human pilot anymore.

One of their spacecraft is called the space Toyger, this spacecraft can fly you anywhere in space.

It's been to every planet in the solar system, one of the times it came under attack by an alien spacecraft.

It shot off a few hypersonic missiles, that hit the alien spacecraft causing it to blow up.

The Air Force has 3,072 fighter jets and 1,800 special attack helicopters and 75 scouting helicopters. They also have 200 multi use jets, that transform into submarines.

It took alien engineers a year to complete this special jet, and these jets rarely break down. The propulsion systems are like no other because they're airtight.

While it's under the water it can travel up to 100 knots. When in the sky it can do Mach 5.

8 of the scouting helicopters were badly damaged, and 2 of them wouldn’t start up because of multiple transmission issues.

Sabastian ordered both the helicopters to be scrapped and mentioned to his Air

Force engineers to get working on a new advanced space bomber.

He wants the bomber to be completed in 8 months. All of the naval ships are even controlled by artificial intelligence.

There are a total of 2,329 advanced stage 4 stealth ships in the naval fleet and 2,000 multi-purpose submarines that can fly.

There are 4 stealth stages, As 4 being top of the stages. A 4th staged stealth ship can become invisible for up to 2 hours.

The Ship can do 15 different maneuvers and has 5 different weapons systems on board.

If the artificial intelligence thinks that it's going to lose a battle it goes into doom mode and it'll shoot all of its weapons off at once at the enemy.

All of the Air Force's pilots and sailor's, now work at the several missile manufacturing plants and a plasma cannon manufacturing plant, where their hours are 9 to 5.

The captains of the ships oversee the workers at the missile manufacturing plants. One of the sailors collapsed and refused to continue working.

He was quickly taken away by the guard and dropped off at 1 of the 8 reeducation camps.

A guard at the reeducation camp opened the doors to a building and threw him into it.

Where there were 5 other people sitting on the floor, a man spoke out saying whatever they tell you to do you must do.

"Is there any water around here to drink?"

"No," there's not they took the water bowl away from us.

"What made them take away the water dish?"

"One of us was complaining about sores on our back."

Brandon, used to stay in this building too, but he died after being forced to work continuously for 10 hours.

"Has anyone been able to escape this place?"

"No," someone tried but they were killed.

When you're out in the courtyard don't get near any fences, or there's a chance that you'll be beat by a guard.

I never knew these camps existed until I was brought here, you may never make it out of here alive.

"How long have all of you been here?"

"We've been here for two years."

There's no way that this kind of camp is legal, I got news for you it's legal. The ruler of the world is harsh and can do whatever he wants, with anyone.

"The other day a group of people were sent into the gas chamber."

"What made the guards do that to them?"

"They probably broke the law."

"How many laws must be followed around here?"

"A dozen of them."

If you spit on a guards face they'll cut off one of your fingers, I've observed that happen twice so far. Both people that lost their fingers died from infection 2 weeks later.

I used to love to go on my phone and look at stuff on it all day. I had so many followers on my social media pages, and now I no longer have a phone to go on my social media pages anymore.

"What's that sound coming from outside?"

"It's one of the 15 surveillance drones that monitor us 24/7."

"Did you ever see a guard with a phone?"

"No," they're not permitted to carry a phone.

"What happens if one of us destroys a surveillance drone?"

"Then you'll be put to death."

All the punishments around here are awfully horrific.

“Why’s that man sitting in the corner chained to a pole?”

“He tried to bite one of the guards.”

He's blind, and he’ll sometimes walk into things or go places he shouldn't be. The worst thing about this place is that if you’re a Christian and the people around here find out you'll be prosecuted.

I've been a Christian all of my life, and I had to change my religion just to survive another day in this place.

“What can I choose to be then?”

“You can choose to be an atheist or a satanist, and that's the only 2 choices that you're given.”

I chose to be an atheist, and you should too. Okay I'm going to take your word on that and become an atheist.

Legend has it that satan, lives on his throne under this very ground that we're standing on.

A few months ago, there were many children brought here, they were all very frightened and they were taken somewhere by the satanist group.

All I could hear was screaming, coming from the woodland area just outside of the fence. After that day I had nightmares for 3 days. There were 10 children, and I've come to believe that they were sacrificed.

"Did any of the guards talk about what happened that day?"

“No,” because they have to keep their mouths shut.

“What were your dreams about?”

“They were about a kind of reptilian that would chase me around this place.”

“Did you fight back in your dream?”

“No,” I didn’t.

“What's that siren going off for?”

“That means that it's dinnertime, and if you get to the dining hall too late they won't serve you.”

## Chapter 2

I know that because that happened to someone that I know in this place. Just come with me and I'll show you where to go.

"Do you see the group of people standing over there in the courtyard with the red hats on?"

"Yes," they're the group of satanists that took the children away into the woods, but don't start any kind of fights with them.

Eventually they came to the dining hall, the smell of fresh bread wafted through the room. The guy sitting in the corner with the spiked hair is trouble, he's a food thief.

"Is that why he's handcuffed to the table?"

"Yes," and he can get very violent towards others.

They entered the food line; you can only have 3 food entries. Like for instance I'm going to have turkey, a tomato, and a piece of bread.

I'm going to get the same, after exiting the line they sat down at a table together. There's such a chill in the air, it's always like that in these buildings.

Every Friday at 2:00 PM the big boss shows up. He's not a very nice person, and I suggest that you don't talk to him.

"Whys that?"

"Because then he'll interrogate you."

There's never been a day that he's been happy, one day when he came here, he killed 2 people that he didn't like.

A few mice scurried past them; a lot of people here like to feed them. They finished eating and put there trays back, the bread tasted better then everything else that I ate.

Suddenly the ground began to shake, they were taken by a guard outside to a work site.

The guard shouted out you're all expected to work out here for 5 hours, your water dishes are on they're on their way.

“Aren’t they going to give us cups to put the water in?”

“No,” they don't do that here.

Eventually they brought them their water dishes and everyone took a drink. He thought to himself I hope that this water isn't contaminated with poison.”

“What are we making here anyway?”

“We're not making anything were just smashing concrete.”

This job is strenuous, and only a strong person can survive doing this every day.

Suddenly the ground broke apart 100 feet away from them. Fire came up through the crack in the earth, look there's something going on over there.

"Maybe you should tell the guard about what's going on over there?"

"No," let them find out for themselves.

Quickly get back to work before the guards come over here. Then 2 more cracks opened up in the earths surface, the hand of a demon came up out of the hole.

The demon pulled himself out of the ground, and when it saw the drones fireballs formed in his hands. He threw the balls at the drones causing them to explode in midair.

Many guards saw this happening and got down out of the towers and ran towards the action.

> "Do you think they're going to unchain us from this pole so that we can escape the demons?"
>
> "No," they're not going to do that.

There was constant fire going on around them, the guards were going up against 4 enraged demons. One of the demons grabbed a guard by his throat and slit his throat with his sharp nails.

Another guard was shooting at 2 demons at the same time, the one demon ripped the weapon out of his hands and stabbed his sharp claws into his chest.

The key to the shackles fell out of his pocket, one of the prisoners took this opportunity and quickly snatched up the keys.

The prisoners quickly opened up all of their shackles, they happened to run past a building with a large window in it. Where they saw a prisoner sitting in a chair, with 3 tubes going to his brain.

Don't worry about that guy we need to get out of here, I'm sure he'll get out of there soon.

They quickly stepped over a fence that was knocked over by the demons. Moments later a 10-foot-tall demon king came up out of the ground in the middle of the camp.

With his massively strong fists he crushed several of the guards. Then he crushed part of the experimental prisoner building, the prisoner in there quickly tore the 3 hoses from his head and ran away and never looked back.

The demon king flattened out all the buildings in the camp, then the entire ground collapsed downward exposing the entrance to the underworld.

The demon king shouted out join me my winged demons, 2 winged demons flew up out of the ground. Somehow a satanist survived and was observing everything.

One of the winged demons saw the human and swooped down grabbing him by the shoulders with his sharp claws and dropped him into the opening in the earth.

His body burned up and immediately turned into a demon. The demon king closed his eyes and suddenly went into a meditative state.

He could hear the thoughts of the millions of satanist's around the world. Hearing all the thoughts strengthened him, both winged demons were struck by lightning bolts. The demon king opened his eyes and roared.

Arch angel Michael was alerted by God's Angel that the earth was under attack by the demon king. Michael came down from the heavens with a mighty roar of thunder and once he landed he drew his godly sword.

The demon king laughed, how dare you come down and try to stop me. I'm too strong for you to defeat me, we'll see about that.

I'm not going to allow you to take innocent souls to strengthen yourself anymore. You enslave humans to traffic children, then you scare them to death and kill them and drink there blood.

What's worst of all you had your demons disguising themselves as humans and they taught God's children that innocence is a bad thing. I know all your weaknesses and I'll use them against you, your days are numbered evil one. The demon kings guards rose up out of the ground around where he stood.

Your guards are weak and they don't scare me. 2 guardian angels came down from heaven and stood beside Michael. I'm so much stronger than your puny angels are, I'll easily defeat them.

Michael swung his sword, hitting one of the demon guards, causing him to turn into dust. Eventually he defeated all of the demons guards and went after the 11-foot-tall demon king.

The demon king's hands went on fire, and flames shot out of his chest at Michael, he immediately ducked.

Before the demon was ready to attack again Michael swung his sword cutting off his head. The demon king's body immediately turned to stone, and Michael lifted up the stone and threw it into the hole in the earth.

Moments later the hole filled in, and Michael and both guardian angels returned to heaven. The prisoners continued to run through the woods until they came to a city.

2 prisoners had stolen money from 3 of the dead guards, Both prisoners went into a clothing shop and bought several clothes for the other prisoners who were very gracious for the new clothes. They even bought one another food, after that they went their separate ways.

## Chapter 3

Meanwhile in a laboratory in Greece, the scientists were testing the brain machine. They did a few tests, and the machine did everything that it was supposed to do. The lead scientist called Sabastian, who was expecting his call.

Hello Trey, it's nice to hear from you today. Tell me all about the brain machine that you have.

The machine is made from a few different components, it functions better than I thought it would.

"How does it attach to someone's head?"

"3 hoses and the metal piece."

"How long do you think it would take you to make enough of these brain machines to connect them to everyone’s brain?”

“12 months.”

That's not the time frame that I was thinking of if you can speed things up. There's not even enough room to fit that many machines in this laboratory.

Then find a manufacturing plant nearby and get started making these machines there.

If any of the workers get in your way just throw them out, if they give you any flak tell them I told you so.

Your job when we hang up is going to be to make me a list of all materials that you’ll be needing.

Then I'll order all the materials for you, and I'll have the shipments rushed to you. You can share what we just talked about with your staff, make sure that no one says anything bad about me.

There's a lot of people out there that want me dead, I understand that. You used to tell me about your family every day that you talked to me on the phone.

I haven't talked about them because my mother isn't doing so well, the one World Health care system is failing us, like it is many others. She needs an important medication but doesn't have thousands of dollars to pay the copay for it.

The doctor believes that she should do assisted suicide, they keep trying to convince her to do it, but I won't allow it.

I’ve been working extra shifts and putting away money to help her pay for it. You know that I'd like to help you but I can't, I've heard that from you many times.

It wouldn't hurt anything to help a fellow human being in need, we'll see what happens after you have finished all the brain machines.

Your such a cold heartless person, you're not the only one that said that about me. I don’t want to hang on the phone with you for much longer.

While you and I are talking thousands of people are being murdered in your re-education camps.

I heard that there's going to be another war between us and two other alien planets. You've heard right, but of course we're going to be victorious again. I think that you better change the health care system, no I'm not going to do that.

Thousands of people are dying because they can't afford their medication, when you sit back on your throne and have every kind of medication known to man at your fingertips.

You just wait until I pay you a visit next time, I'll be giving you a good thrashing. You're threats don't scare me, mark my words one day you're going to be assassinated. When you go to the meetings with the friendly aliens you treat them so badly.

You rarely give them a chance to finish saying with their opinion is. You took away our freedom of speech, you shouldn't be allowed to have freedom of speech anymore either.

Just keep talking I'm going to write down everything that you're saying about me, and I may have you thrown into a camp after your work is done.

Your secret military came out and disarmed us from all of our weapons, in the middle of the night.

I'm comfortable knowing that none of you will be coming after me with a gun. I'm currently looking at my guns while we're speaking to one another. I haven't shot my guns in a while, suddenly there was a bang.

Guard, please get this animal out of my room, don't let any animal get in here again or I'm going to shoot one of you.

"What was that all about?"

"My Guards weren't watching out like they should have been."

"What kind of animal was it?"

"A Mountain Lion."

"Do you realize were at 100% green energy?"

"No," and I don't care about that.

You and I have wasted enough time chatting, I'll talk to you later bye now. Now to a chip manufacturing plant in Europe, it was just a typical day there. All the workers were keeping themselves busy, when 2 of the workers walked in holding the crowbars, shouting no more government. The other workers just ignored them, until one of the men whacked one of the workers in the back with the crowbar.

The guards must have heard the commotion from outside and came inside to face the intruders. They fired their guns at the 2 men, but they dove behind a machine.

Both men were trying to make their way out of the plant, while they were getting shot at. Both men were able to escape, even being chased by armed guards. The guard shouted out when you're found you're going to be killed.

Suddenly a borage of missiles came out of the sky and struck the left side of the building.

The 10 workers that were working on that side of the building were blown apart. The guards helped everyone to evacuate the building, afterwards the guards attempted to put the fire out in the plant. They quickly called the fire department, who arrived as quickly as they could.

After quite some time they were able to put out the fire, and the guards and the workers could return to the building. 10 months later Trey and his team finished building the 4 million brain machines and delivered them to underground laboratories all over the world.

Leven was working as a carpenter, at the time when Sabastian's mercenaries came for him as well as the rest of the population. Every one's cell phone were taken away from them and thrown into a pile.

Anyone that had credit cards had their cards taken from them and burned up. Everyone's paper dollars were taken from them and thrown into a burn barrel.

The people were told that the reason the paper money was taken from them was because the leader outlawed paper money making a digital currency instead.

# Chapter 4

Everyone's identification cards were taken from them, while this was happening several surveillance drones were in the air.

They were given cards with numbers on them, then a fist fight broke out between the guard and young man.

The guard took a punch to the chin, then immediately retaliated by punching the kid in the ribs.

Out of nowhere an assassinated drone came overhead of the boy, using its artificial intelligence it scanned the boy and knew everything about him. It said the fighter must be eliminated and shot him.

Suddenly all the mercenaries put on their gas masks, 110 massive long range cargo planes flew over the entire planet releasing sleeping gas.

Within minutes the entire population collapsed, falling asleep. The people were then taken down into an underground tunnel, that spanned around the entire earth.

Some of the guards in the underground tunnel had been experimented on and sometimes have vampiric tendencies. These guards never come out of the tunnel to see the light of day.

The normal guards carry around a crystal called a Bloomin, which keeps them safe from the vampire guards at night.

Sabastian has met with these vampire guards a few times, while the tunnels were being created a rare race of crystal people were disturbed. They're 7 feet tall, and their skin is orange.

If a human gets too close to them, then they receive a shock. All the crystal people were very angry and talking in their language at the human guards.

Who didn't understand a word that they were saying, so they stepped back and let the vampire guards go over to the crystal people because they understood their language.

After talking to each other for a while, the vampire guards got the crystal people to calm down.

Afterwards the guards called Sabastian and mentioned to him about the crystal people that they came upon.

Sabastian put the crystal people on a reserve to live out their days. Many days later the people who were put to sleep woke up and found themselves in laboratories with three hoses connected to their heads.

Right beside them was a health monitoring machine and there was a chart on the wall that said good and bad thinking. Leven, Alvarez, and Sardis we're all in the same room together.

Windel, Arrigo, and Chibuogu we're held in the room next door. Chantel was in the brain mapping machine.

While there were guards standing on either side of her, she was feeling a bit claustrophobic.

A minute later a lab technician came over next to her, just to see how she was doing and seeing how the mapping was going.

"Chantel yelled out how much longer is this going to take?"

"Another 20 minutes."

"Where will I be going after this?"

"To the brain chamber."

"Can't we just skip putting me in there?"

"No," or we're going against protocol.

"Will I be able to eat after leaving the brain chamber?"

"Yes," and you'll be eating a brain protein bar.

We're giving you that because you don't have enough brain proteins at the moment. What you're talking about just went way over my head, it means that for some reason your body has slowed in the brain protein making department.

"How many proteins are in our brain?"

"222."

You're now free to exit the brain mapping machine, and then the guards escorted her down 2 long hauls to the brain chamber.

The chamber was lit up in purple, and there were white dots on the wall of the chamber.

Then another technician sat her down in a chair and placed an ertina head band over her head.

I'm going to be going over a procedure with you right now, this will help us get the best results from the headband.

I want you to do 5 different things for me, I want you to blink your left eye two times and your right eye once. I'll give you 2 minutes to do that and then we'll move on to the next thing.

After the two minutes are done, now make a fist with your right hand and blink both eyes 10 times. That's very good now we're moving on to the next thing.

Close both your eyes and just open your right eye, and frown. I'd like you to do that 3 times, you did that very efficiently. Now you just have 2 more movements to do for me.

I want you to turn your neck to the left and blink your right eye. Finally, we're at the last objective I want you to do.

Bring both your arms over your head and just blink your left eye 5 times for me. The technician held a small tablet up in front of her face, I'm going to play 2 sounds to you.

Tell me which one of the 2 sounds that you hear then, okay here's sound one. Wait for 2 minutes and then you'll hear the sound, 2 minutes went by and she didn't hear a thing.

Now we're going on to the second sound, it took her 3 minutes to hear this sound. It's typical for a woman not to hear the first sound, the men normally hear the first sound.

"Can I please stop the testing?"

"Yes," you may.

"What are you feeling exactly?"

"I'm feeling dizzy and my left eye is hurting me and I have a headache."

I don't like that you're having 3 symptoms at once, if you take this red pill you'll feel better within 5 minutes.

"Do you even know what's in this red pill?"

"I know of some things that are in it but I don't know everything that's in it."

If you refuse to take it then I can't make you. The technician quickly took out a syringe and stabbed it in her arm. The stuff that went into her veins, it had 40% alien brain cells in it, with 20% winnta, not much is known about this medication.

4 % of lizard stem cells, and 2% human brain cells. Alvarez suddenly went into a dream, and his legs began shaking.

One of the guards walked over to him and tapped him on the shoulder, waking him from his vivid dream. While Sardis, beat up the guards that were escorting him to another room.

He took both guards guns and waited for more guards to come so that he could kill them.

5 minutes later 3 more guards rushed into the room and he shot them on the spot. He took some ammunition from the dead guards, and proceeded to the next room, where he shot 2 more guards dead.

When he saw a vampire guard he hid behind a desk so he wouldn't be seen by him.

He got out from behind the desk and peeked out the doorway, he saw that the vampire  guard was drinking the blood from the dead guards.

Windel busted out of his chair that he was tied down to using a sharp scissors that he found.

He too began killing the guards, who found himself face to face with a vampire guard. Whom he killed with his silver knife; Sardis opened a secret door and ran as fast as he could to the end of the passageway.

2 hours later he came to the 5th passageway and killed the 3 guards that were there.

He came to a ladder and climbed up it and came to a hatch that led to Sabastian's personal home. Out of nowhere came a fierce ninja, Sardis shot at him but he was too nimble and dodged the bullet.

The ninja swung his sword but missed Sardis and struck a shelf. Sardis shot the ninja in the side, killing him then another ninja joined in.

The ninja threw 2 throwing knives at him, which he was able to dodge. Sardis saw that there was a throwing star on the shelf beside him, he quickly grabbed it and threw it at the ninja.

Hitting him in the leg, but still, this didn't stop the ninja from attacking. He did a spinning wheel kick and hit the ninja right in the face, knocking him backwards into the wall.

He grabbed his gun from the floor and shot the ninja two times in the chest, his body slumped over. He could hear something coming his way, the door swung open and it was a robotic attack dog. He immediately opened fire on it before it could get too close to him.

The thin layer of armor covering the dogs body was no match for the armor piercing bullets.

Sparks flew from the dog's body and it collapsed, before entering the next room he peeked around the corner to see what else may be waiting for him in there.

Before stepping forward, he noticed the tripwire. He went back to the previous room that he was just in and began searching the room for wire cutters.

He saw that there were a chest of drawers in the corner of the room, he opened the first drawer and found a pair of wire cutters.

When he turned to see what the buzzing sound was, it was a drone. He raised his gun and shot at the drone, but the drone was able to outmaneuver the bullets. It fired two darts at him, he swung his body around and the darts missed him.

He grabbed 2 books off of the shelf next to him and threw them at the drone, one of the books hit the drone knocking it down.

Then he went back to tending to the tripwire, there were three different colored wires.

He cut the wire that was the middle disarming the bomb. He placed the long wire that he just cut in his pocket.

He could hear someone walking down the steps, and quickly darted into the next room, in this room there was a bathroom then he went into to hide from whoever was coming.

The guard entered the room, he was holding an automatic weapon. Sardis swung open the door surprising the guard and opened fire on him, hitting him in the neck killing him. Another guard that was upstairs heard the gunfire and rushed down the steps.

When he entered the room, he noticed the dead guard. Sardis took the long wire out of his pocket; he attacked the guard by punching him in the face, when the guard tried to swing back he wrapped the wire around his throat.

He tried to go for his gun but Sardis tightened the wire around his throat, causing the guard to collapse and stop breathing.

Sardis took a knife from the guard and carefully and quietly walked along the side of the stairway. He swung the rifle over his shoulder and was holding a knife.

Once at the top of the stairs there was a darkened hallway off to his right. He entered a room that was off to his left, in the room there was a bed and a walk-in closet.

There was a big mirror in the back of the room, with a small crack in it. He could smell a slight scent of perfume, coming from the clothes that were on the floor in the corner.

Above the bed there was a cross hanging there, on the right side of the cross was a fist sized hole in the wall.

He could hear music playing in the room next to him, this made him on guard. He quietly walked out of the room but didn't go around the corner.

He knew that soon someone may be coming out of the room, suddenly the door to the room next door opened.

It was a guard in full tactical gear, and a woman wearing all black. The woman proceeded down the hallway towards him.

Once she came around the corner he grabbed her and placed his hand over her mouth.

In sign language he told her to be quiet and had her go into the room and he closed the door and locked it.

The guard asked, "Where are you baby?"

When there was no response he made his way down the hall.

We don't have time to play hide and seek together, in an angered voice he said get out here now.

He drew his pistol and turned on the laser sight. Sardis waited for the right time and struck the guard in the neck with his knife, killing him.

The woman that he locked in the room became angry and began trying to open the door but realized that it was locked. Sardis walked to the end of the hall, and off to his right there was a door.

He opened this door and saw that there was another flight of steps that went up or down.

He could hear someone coming up the steps, this time it was a vampire guard. He quickly went to the right side of the door when the guard was about to walk through the doorway.

The moment the guard walked in the doorway he forcefully pushed him backwards, causing him to fall down 2 flight of stairs.

This didn't faze him much because he’s a vampire, Sardis saw the blade he was carrying had a silver blade.

The vampire came right up the steps again, and this time he stabbed the vampire three times in the neck.

He dragged the vampires body into the room next to him and closed the door. He went into the stairwell and went up the steps to the third floor.

He came upon a large living room area, on the leather couch there was a dead man's body lying there. There was blood splattered all over the walls, he continued down another hall.

At the end of the hall there was a door, he slowly opened the door. When he entered there was a man sitting in a chair, that was facing the other way.

Sabastian was sitting there and was all drugged up. Sardis opened fire on him, emptying his clip into him. After killing Sabastian, he found his way out of the mansion.

He stole one of the trucks that were outside and took off for parts unknown. Chantel's arms grew in size and she grew a set of fangs, and her fingernails grew into claws.

Her hearing was heightened, and her sense of smell was improved. She looked over at the technician who was trying to hide behind a shelf.

She grabbed the technician by the throat and sunk her fangs into her chest killing her. Chantel busted through several walls and found her way up and out of the tunnel.

As she was walking along, Sardis came driving along. He pulled over and let her get into the truck, when he got a good look at her, he saw how terrifying she looked but didn't seem to care.

They talked about how they escaped to one another, and that's when both of them decided to go all around the world to bust people out of the places that they were held.

A day later Leven, Alvarez, Windel, Arrigo, and Chibuogu were rescued by Sardis and Chantel. It took a long time to find and rescue the rest of the people in the world.

www.ingramcontent.com/pod-product-compliance
Lightning Source LLC
La Vergne TN
LVHW050343160826
845677LV00014B/3755
*9798370730474*